Blood
Brothers

Book Three
Pigeon Hollow Mysteries

Samantha Jillian Bayarr

ATTENTION READER: If you have not read the first TWO books in this series, this book will not make sense to you, as it is a continuation in the series. Please take the time to read Book One: The Amish Girl, and Book Two: Sins of the Father, for the best reading experience.

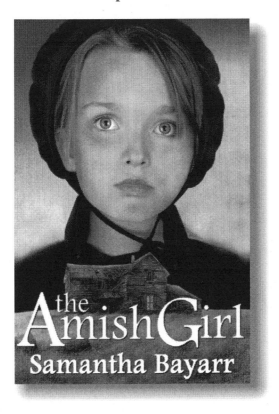

Book Two

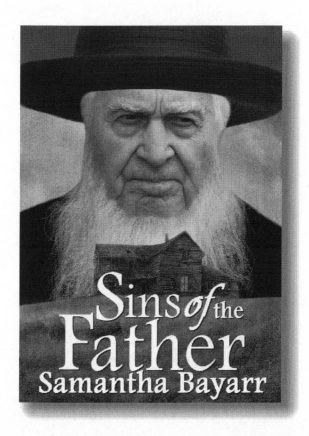

Sins *of* the
Father
Samantha Bayarr

A note from the Author:

While this novel is set against the backdrop of an
Amish community, the characters and the names of
the community are fictional. There is no intended
resemblance between the characters in this book or
the setting, and any real members of any Amish or
Mennonite community. As with any work of
fiction, I've taken license in some areas of research
as a means of creating the necessary circumstances
for my characters and setting. It is completely
impossible to be accurate in details and
descriptions, since every community differs, and
such a setting would destroy the fictional quality of
entertainment this book serves to present. Any
inaccuracies in the Amish and Mennonite lifestyles
portrayed in this book are completely due to
fictional license. Please keep in mind that this book
is meant for fictional, entertainment purposes only,
and is not written as a text book on the Amish.

Happy Reading

Chapter 1

"He asked to see the Bishop," Caleb told Kyle.

"Do you trust him?"

"I think we have no choice. I believe he wants to confess to the Bishop before he turns himself in. He told me he knows he needs to pay for the crimes he committed."

"Do you think it's wise to take him back home? I'm not sure any of us are safe," Kyle said nervously.

"I know he's done wrong, and he agrees he needs to turn himself in, but he's our father, and I think we should let him speak to the Bishop first."

"I suppose you're right," Kyle agreed. "But do you really think he should be around my mom and Amelia?"

"They're safe and sound at your house with the doors locked, and we removed all his guns from his house. Besides, it's only for an hour while he meets with the Bishop."

They waited outside the same locked room Kyle's mom had occupied only two days before, while the nurse slid her card in the lock to release him.

Zeb Yoder took his time in meeting them in the hallway, not seeming interested in leaving the hospital psychiatric ward.

"We have a search warrant to search the premises, and we brought a crew to dig up the grave your father buried some years ago. He's claimed it's empty, but there are laws against this sort of thing, whether the casket is empty or not."

Kyle and Caleb looked at the five-man crew wearing reflective vests and toting shovels, who stood behind the two police officers.

"We're going to need your father to go with us out to the grave site."

"He's in the middle of a meeting with our Bishop right now, can you wait a few minutes?"

"I'm afraid we're on a schedule," the officer said. "The city is paying these men to be here, and the city won't pay for your father to finish his visit."

"I'll get him," Caleb said.

Kyle's nerves jangled while he listened to the men grumble about the Amish thinking they are *above the law.* He leered at them, wishing he could blend away from the scene that was about to unfold, but even he was curious about the casket that was buried at the back of the old man's property.

When Caleb returned with his father, the Bishop agreed to go with him for support, and Caleb thought it was more out of curiosity than anything else. Surely the rest of the community would hear about all of this before it even hit the newspapers.

One of the officers asked Zeb to step outside on the porch. "Are you Zebedee Yoder?"

He nodded. "*Jah.*"

The officer pulled out a pair of handcuffs and proceeded to read him his rights.

"What are you doing?" Kyle asked.

The officer ignored Kyle until he was finished. "Do you understand these rights?"

Zeb nodded again.

"Your father is under arrest for unlawful and improper burial, and for violating the city and county ordinances regarding placement of graves."

Knowing Zeb had committed far worse crimes than this, Kyle still wanted to make sure the man was being charged fairly. "But the grave is empty!"

"That doesn't matter!" the officer said. "There are codes and regulations regarding burials of anything other than house-pets, and your father broke the law."

"But he didn't bury anything other than a casket!" Kyle continued to argue. "What's the harm in that?"

Why was he defending the man? Did his blood-tie to the man suddenly shift his thoughts to have compassion for him even after all he'd done?

"Let's go dig up the casket so we can be sure it's empty," the officer said, ignoring Kyle.

After everything that had happened, Kyle had to admit he was just as curious to see if it was empty.

"Is that *really* against the law?" Caleb whispered to his brother.

Kyle shrugged, as they followed the officers out to the site. "I've heard of some strange laws on the books, so who knows. But I'm thinking they should have brought a back-hoe to dig it up. They're going to have fun cutting through the frozen ground with those shovels."

When they reached the site, one of the men removed the grave marker, a nice cross Caleb had carved for his mother, and tossed it to the ground. Upset by this, he went over to retrieve it, and was told to leave it since it was evidence. This angered him since he'd planned to have a proper burial for his mother, and that cross would serve as a grave marker wherever they put her.

The men began to dig, and everyone else stood by and watched. The tension was thick, anticipation making everyone's nerves stand on edge. The men made light work of digging up the shallow grave, each man taking his methodical turn as if they did this all the time.

When the primitive box was unearthed, they brushed it off and pulled it from the shallow grave.

"It's heavy," one of them said, turning to Zeb. "I thought you said this casket was empty!"

"I had a funeral for my wife—for my son's sake, so he wouldn't know his mother had chosen to leave him," he protested.

Caleb cringed.

More lies.

Aenti Selma had told him that Zeb had forbidden his mother to see him again. Did his father even know the truth anymore?

"Open it up!" the officers ordered the men.

Two of them used their shovels to pry open the casket. When they flipped open the lid, they all cringed and backed away, holding their hands over their faces and groaning, but Kyle and Caleb were not close enough to see what the problem was.

As the wind shifted, the stench of death consumed them.

All eyes peered in to see the deceased, fully clad in an Amish dress and *kapp*.

Chapter 2

Kyle felt his legs buckle underneath his six-foot frame.

What kind of man was this who shared his DNA?

He blew out a hard breath, watching the icy puff of air crystalize and evaporate, as if that was all he could concentrate on at the moment.

Did he dare look at the body? Did it even matter?

She was there no matter if he looked or not. Nothing was going to change the fact that his own father had committed such an unspeakable act.

His gaze traveled to Caleb, his *brother,* who had collapsed, and was sitting in the snow. He reached a shaky hand to him, but the muffled chaos around the grave switched his thoughts toward the men.

He felt his brother's hand in his, but he didn't turn. He couldn't turn away from the sight of the open casket, despite the tugging from Caleb's hand as he struggled to his feet.

With his brother beside him now, the two walked slowly toward the open casket, and the crowd of men who'd gathered there. Pictures flashed; orders were barked. One of the officers stepped away and radioed for the coroner and backup officers to come to the scene.

A perimeter of bright yellow tape was wound around two adjacent trees, roping off the *crime scene.*

Kyle couldn't think straight. His mind reeled with the possibility that the woman in that casket could have been his own mother. He wondered what Caleb must be thinking, knowing they were about to unearth his mother's grave as soon as the warrant was signed. Surely it would be signed now that a new *body* had turned up unexpectedly.

More pictures flashed, and Kyle shuddered at the thought of what the newspaper headlines would say. His name would be linked to this crime, now that Old Man Yoder had confessed to being his father.

He watched in horror as the old man protested, claiming he had no idea how the body had gotten into the casket, while they read him his rights again.

Accused of *murder.*

It held a certain stigma Kyle wasn't certain he would ever be able to shake. No one ever thinks such a thing could happen in their own family, but now he'd been grandfathered into this family and all of its problems.

He silently wished he'd never come back to Pigeon Hollow looking for answers. Wished he'd never made that delivery to Amelia and Caleb that day.

But that wasn't fair. It wasn't fair to them, since he cared so much for them both. Not to mention the fact that he'd have never found his mother if he hadn't come back. He certainly would never have known he had a brother. But at what price had all that come to him?

Kyle turned to Caleb, who was weeping.

Swallowing down the lump in his throat, he felt the warmth of a tear that rapidly froze against his own cheek, and it startled him.

How could he be so happy to have a brother, yet feel so miserable to be related to him? It confused him how both feelings could consume him all at once.

Kyle peered into the casket, unable to fight his curiosity any longer. His blood ran cold when the realization hit him. Though she was mostly unrecognizable, due to decay, the frozen earth had preserved her enough for him to know exactly who she was.

But how?

"Aunt Miriam," he whispered.

Chapter 3

Caleb turned to Kyle, horror spread across his face. "You know that woman?" He asked.

Kyle focused on his brother's face, his heart racing, dizziness overcoming him. He felt the bile rise up in his throat, and tried to swallow it down, but it was determined to escape. He turned his head and stepped to the side, leaning over and retching up the contents of his stomach. He coughed and choked and sputtered, until his stomach was empty. Then, he used his foot to kick fresh snow over the mess, and quickly grabbed a handful and wiped it across his mouth, not caring just how cold it was. He flicked the ice and water from his hand and then drew his sleeve across his mouth to wipe it dry.

Caleb approached him and placed a hand on his brother's back just to let him know he was there. Kyle turned a half turn toward him, feeling a little embarrassed.

"Are you alright, big brother?"

Kyle sniffled and nodded, wiping his eyes with his palms. If not for the crowd that still remained at the gravesite, he would have walked away, but his aunt awaited identification, and right now he was the only one who could identify her.

He had to pull himself together for her sake. Then there would be the task of calling uncle Jack and his cousins—a family it turned out he wasn't really related to.

Did they even know she'd been gone?

He hadn't seen his *cousin,* Seth, in the six years since he'd left their home to go out on his own. He'd seen the twins, Ellen and Elizabeth, but both had families of their own now, and he'd fallen away from the entire family.

His mother and his *Aunt* Miriam had been friends, and she'd mentioned them leaving home together during their *rumspringa*. What he couldn't wrap his mind around, was the connection to the old man, or why they'd found her buried on his property. Kyle was determined to find out the sordid details, no matter how much worse things got for them.

One of the officers approached Kyle, while the other closed Zeb in the back of the patrol car. Strangely, the old man was emotionless—as if he lacked a conscience. Kyle had very little faith in his father. But even after all the old man had put him through, he still felt a twinge of sadness at having never known him.

He shuddered, swallowing down the thought.

Blood ties did not make him feel any less estranged from his father, but those ties came with the burden of bearing a certain amount of responsibility; a responsibility he did not want.

"Did I hear you say you know this woman?" the officer asked Kyle.

Kyle blew out his breath, trying his best to understand what the officer had said to him. The pounding of his heartbeat had muffled the question, and drowned out everything around him.

"Young man," the officer said, placing a hand on Kyle's shoulder.

The action startled him, bringing the foreground to life.

"I asked you a question. Can you identify this woman?"

Kyle nodded methodically, finding it difficult to concentrate. "I—I think I do. I think she's a woman I've known all my life as my aunt."

He knew his mother would not be the best one to identify her, since they hadn't seen each other in so many years. But even if she was, he would spare his mother the gruesome task.

"My *Uncle* Jack," Kyle found himself saying. "Or maybe one of my *cousins,* would be the best ones to tell you for sure."

"Where can I find these family members?"

"I don't know for sure," he said, trying to remember their new address. He'd only been there once, but it was possible he could find it again. When he'd last seen the twins, they were out shopping in downtown Hartford, and had told him briefly about the trouble Seth had been involved with, and his drinking and gambling problems, but they had been in a hurry that day, and they'd each promised to keep in touch. Sadly, it hadn't happened.

"It's been a few years since I've seen any of them, but they're over in Hartford."

"That's still part of Raven County," the officer said without emotion. "So we can look into it further. Give me their full names and the approximate location, and we can track them down for you."

Kyle felt sick again.

"Maybe—I should be the one to talk to them," he said.

"I'm sorry, but this is a police matter now. We'll handle it."

After giving the officer his own information, Kyle and Caleb went up to the old man's house to get some coffee, and to get out of the cold that had numbed them both beyond the reality of the unearthed body.

They walked past the Bishop, but he lowered his gaze, and that was enough to let them know the ban would never be lifted for their family.

Chapter 4

Kyle rang the doorbell of his Uncle Jack's home, shaking uncontrollably at the words he'd rehearsed, but had suddenly left him. He struggled to remember just what it was he was going to say, and how he was going to say it. That wasn't something you blurted out on the street. He'd have to wait until he'd had a chance to be welcomed in by his uncle, and made sure the man was sitting down when he gave him the news.

Lost in thought, he suddenly realized the door had opened, and an older woman he didn't know was standing on the stoop, staring at him. Her brow furrowed over her dark eyes, and the gray, disheveled hair matched her complexion.

"Do I have to call the police," she was saying to him. "Or are you going to get off my porch willingly?"

She swatted at him with the broom in her hand, and he took a step back, almost falling backward off the icy slab of cement.

He grabbed onto the iron, stair rail to keep from toppling down the steps. "I'm looking for my Uncle Jack—Jack Sinclair," he said, finally finding his voice.

"I bought this place fair and square," she said, narrowing her gaze at him. "And not you, or that other man, is going to run me off!"

Horror spread across his face. "What *other* man?" he asked.

"That old, Amish man!" she answered.

Kyle could feel bile rising up in his throat again, but pushed it down. "Did he have a long white beard?" he asked, demonstrating the length with his hand. "And a constant angry look on his face?"

She nodded vigorously. "Yeah, that's the one! You kin to that crazy man?"

Not on purpose! he thought.

"I just happen to know who you're talking about. He's done some things—well, that's why I'm looking for my Uncle. I need to tell him my aunt is, um—dead."

Her face grew more ashen. "That old man killed her?"

Kyle swallowed hard. "Maybe—um—I don't know. I just need to know where I can find my Uncle Jack so I can tell him. Does my family still live here?"

"I told you I bought this place fair and square— from Jack Sinclair."

"How long ago?"

"Just before the first snowfall," she said with a far-off look. "I remember it because I was glad I got everything moved before it got too cold and slippery for the movers. I didn't want them to drop any of my things and break them."

"Back in November?" he asked impatiently.

"Yes," she said, nodding her head. "The first day I was in here, that Amish man came looking for him. He accused me of hiding him in my house! He pushed right past me and tracked mud all over my floors. Funniest thing, too—it wasn't even raining that day!"

Probably the day he buried my Aunt Miriam!

"Did he say why he was looking for my Uncle Jack?"

"No! And I didn't ask. I just wanted him to leave, but he showed up again the next day, so I called the police. By the time the police showed up, he was long-gone. He's a scary, scary man!"

I'm aware of that!

"Did my Uncle Jack leave a forwarding address?" he asked the older woman.

"No!" she answered curtly. "I've told you all I'm gonna tell you; now it's time to get off my property."

"Well, thank you for your time."

Kyle walked away, feeling more discouraged and more worried than ever. Things were certainly pointing toward his flesh and blood being a murderer at least two times over, and the very thought of it made his stomach churn.

Hopping in his truck that he'd left parked in front of the building, he looked up one more time at the place in which he'd resided with people he thought were his family. His whole life has been one big lie after another, and he'd hoped that finding his mother alive would be the beginning of good things, but it just wasn't. Having a father who'd committed crimes had opened up a new and bitter world for him. A world he wanted no part of at the moment.

By tomorrow, the news would be smeared all over the papers, and embarrassment would come down on his and Caleb's heads. It certainly wouldn't help their new roofing company at all, but that was the least of his troubles.

Now, he worried what Greta's family would think of him, and if her father would forbid him to continue courting her.

Kyle pulled up to the ranch-style home he'd last known his cousin, Ellen, to live in, and parked his truck close to the door. The place looked abandoned for some time; tall, brown grass poked through the snow, and the door hung from its hinges, the front window broken clean out.

Regardless of the condition of the property, he shouldered out into the wind, and walked carefully over the patches of ice to reach the front door. He knocked loudly on the door, causing it to swing open.

Seeing that the house was empty, except for a bit of trash, and a torn and soiled corduroy recliner in the corner, Kyle felt his hope dwindle. Had the police run into the same roadblocks trying to find his family? For all he knew, they hadn't even begun their search; the old woman he'd just talked to in town would have mentioned if the police had been there.

He looked around the room and blew out a discouraging breath. A small trash can over-flowed with papers in the opposite corner of the room, and Kyle didn't see any harm in looking for a clue to his family's whereabouts.

He made fast work of smoothing out wadded pages of old bills; final notices, and shut-off threats from electric, gas and phone companies took up most of the pile. At the bottom, he found and opened letter with a return address in Florida.

He examined the post-mark, finding it odd that the letter had a cancelled stamp on it from Pigeon Hollow. He read the address again, wondering why the two didn't match. Flipping up the flap of the envelope, he pulled the short letter from inside and read the words that made no sense to him.

"Florida?" he shouted. "She's in Florida?"

He read the short letter once more, thinking there had to be some mistake. There was a return address on the envelope, and he could Google it to see where it was. The post mark was from November, but he couldn't read the exact date.

One thing was certain; the police needed to know this before they told any of his family she might be dead.

Was it possible she was alive in Florida, and he'd mistaken the identity of the woman in the casket?

Chapter 5

"Let go of me!" Seth barked at the officer who was pushing him into the patrol car. "I didn't do anything wrong!"

"For the hundredth time, Mr. Sinclair, it's against the law to drive while under the influence of alcohol."

"And I told *you* at least a hundred times I wasn't driving!" he hollered back. "My friend dropped me off at my car, and I knew I wasn't fit to drive so I decided to call a cab. But I guess I dozed off and I missed him."

"If you hadn't been sleeping in the car, I probably wouldn't have stopped here, but there isn't any overnight parking here. Your car is in a metered zone, and I'm afraid I'm going to have to call a tow truck and have the car impounded too."

"C'mon," he begged. "Please don't do that. I went to a birthday party tonight and celebrated a little too much, but I wasn't driving! You can call my friend *and* the cab company to check out my story. What ever happened to being innocent until proven guilty?"

"You can tell it to the judge when you see him on Monday."

"You mean to tell me I gotta stay in jail all weekend?"

"Unless you can get someone to bail you out before then, but you'll have to wait to make your phone call until after I process you."

"Couldn't you save a little bit of tax-payer's money and let me call the cab company back?"

Before the officer could answer him, a taxi pulled up beside Seth's car.

"There's my cab!" he said. "I told you I wasn't lying!"

The driver jumped out and looked at the officer. "Did one of you call for a cab?" he asked, glancing into the back of the patrol car at Seth. "I would have been here sooner, except that there was a bad accident a few miles back, and traffic is backed up for miles. Looks like about twelve cars involved."

"I told you I called a cab!" Seth said excitedly, as he turned to the officer. "Can you let me go now? You can see I called a cab."

The officer's mouth formed a thin line. "I can see that, but it still doesn't explain how you got here. I arrested you on the suspicion that you were operating the vehicle while intoxicated."

He wanted to ask the officer if that was even legal, but he figured he'd better keep his mouth shut.

"But you looked me up and saw that I've never been arrested before," Seth pleaded with the man.

"For some, that just means they've never been caught!"

"I hate to be rude," the cab driver said. "But if you're going to let him go, I've got a schedule to keep, and I'm sure they could use you down the road at the accident."

The officer turned to Seth and then motioned for him to step out of the back of his patrol car. "I'm going to let you go this time with a warning, but make sure you're better prepared the next time you do a little too much celebrating."

He took the handcuffs off Seth, and then gave him back his license.

"What about my car?" he asked. "Will you give me time to get my friends to pick it up for me. I'm sure it won't take them more than an hour."

He nodded. "As long as it's gone by the time I return from helping with the pile-up back there, then I won't bother with it."

"Thank you, officer," Seth said in his most polite tone. "I'll get them on it right away."

"Have a good night," he said as he got into his patrol car. "Be careful on these icy roads."

"I will," the cab driver said as he waved to the officer.

When he was out of sight, he turned to Seth and waved a finger at him.

"Boy am I glad to see you, Frankie!" Seth said to his friend. "And thanks for not blowing my cover."

"I told you being a cab driver would come in handy one day!"

Seth chuckled as he opened the door to his BMW and grabbed his phone. "I like you better as my *bookie,* but I have to admit, that cab *front* of yours did come in handy!"

"That was pretty slick sending me that text message while the cop was looking up your license!"

"I knew from the look in his eyes he was going to arrest me for something. They see a young guy in a car nicer than what they drive, and they automatically think I've stolen it, or I'm a rich, spoiled punk!"

"Well, I can vouch for you that you're a dirt -poor dude with a good eye for counting cards," he said with a chuckle. "B'cause we grew up on the same side of the tracks!"

"Can I help it if I'm one of the luckiest poker players around?"

"Your luck almost ran out tonight. Don't forget who saved your butt tonight!"

"No chance of that, Frankie, b'cause if I know you, you'll be reminding me for a lot of days to come."

Frankie pulled out his phone and looked up a number. "You should take that act of yours to Vegas and make the two of us some real money, instead of taking these poor suckers around here for a ride all the time."

"You know I can't do that. They'd know I was counting cards, and I'd be arrested for sure," he said, grabbing a cigarette from the pack with his teeth. Then he flicked open his Zippo, striking it with his thumb to light it in one smooth motion.

He held the flame to his cigarette and lit the end, drawing in a smooth stream of smoke and closing his eyes, feeling immediately subdued.

"I thought you said you wanted to quit smoking!" Frankie barked at him as he held his phone to his ear.

"I am," Seth said. "But I need one to calm me down. That cop nearly arrested me—say, who are you calling?"

Frankie looked up. "I'm calling the boys so we can get your car out of here. When that cop gets down the road and figures out that twelve-car pile-up is nothing more than a fender-bender, we might *both* be arrested."

Chapter 6

Frankie hung up the phone and shivered, blowing out a warm breath into the cold night air. "The boys will be here in about ten minutes. Let's sit in the warm car until they get here. I'm freezing!"

"I hope they hurry," Seth said. "Because I want to get out of here before that cop gets back here."

A lone pair of headlights lit up the dark highway just as they were about to get back into the cab.

Frankie looked up. "Too late for that!" he said. "Here he comes now."

"What are we going to do?" Seth asked. "He warned us to get the car out of here before he came back here, and since we didn't, he's going to arrest me!"

Frankie held up a hand hoping to calm his friend. "Now, just give him a chance. He might've come back here just to check up on you. The fact that you didn't get back into your car and drive off should score some points with him. He's not going to arrest you if you're not doing anything wrong."

"I wasn't doing anything wrong the first time!" Seth complained.

"If you keep acting all fidgety, he's going to think something is up, and you *will* get yourself arrested. So calm down."

"Fine," Seth said.

He was already irritable, and the thought of dealing with the police officer again set his teeth on edge.

"What am I supposed to do?" Seth asked with a chuckle. "Act casual? I'm not sure I know how to do that, and I'm not up for going to jail and having to sit there the whole weekend."

"No one's going to jail, if you'd just calm down," Frankie said. "So, yes, you should just act casual."

They watched the officer get out of his car slowly, and Seth could feel his heart racing, his mind reeling with thoughts of how to talk his way out of this one.

"I see you're still sitting here," the officer said as he approached, pointing his question toward Frankie. "I thought you had a schedule to keep."

Frankie chuckled. "Well, when you've got a fare paying you double, you agree to sit wherever that person asks you to."

The officer looked over at Seth. "Double, huh?

Seth nodded methodically.

The officers mouth formed a thin line, and Seth could see he was irritated with the two of them.

"I won't go into the fact that you sent me on a wild goose chase," the officer said calmly. "That twelve-car pileup was nothing more than a little fender bender between two cars. Now, before I get into why you lied to me about that, I'm afraid I'm gonna have to let you know that I need to take you in after all."

Seth's heart slammed against his rib cage. The thought of going to jail didn't sit right with him. He'd been walking the fine line of the law for a while now, but he never thought his actions would land him in jail.

"Why are you arresting me?" he tried to protest. "I didn't do anything wrong. I swear to you I wasn't driving the car. I've been sitting here waiting for my friends to come get it because I didn't want you to take it to the impound yard."

"I'll wait for your friends," he said. "But I'm not arresting you."

"Then why are you taking me in?" Seth asked.

"I'm afraid Son," he said. I'm gonna have to take you in so you can identify a body."

Seth threw his hands up in defense. "A *body!* Wait a minute; I didn't kill anyone!"

"No one said anything about you killing anyone," the officer said. "We've got a Jane Doe, and your name came up as a possible relative to identify the body."

Seth collapsed against his car, his mind reeling with thoughts he didn't want to entertain.

"Are you sure?" he asked. "One of *my* relatives?"

The officer looked at his notes, and then looked back up at Seth, a mournful look clouding his expression. "We have reason to believe the body is that of a Miriam Sinclair".

Seth felt his knees buckle. He couldn't believe it. He refused to believe it.

"That's my mother, but she's alive!"

"The body has been in the ground for some time. When's the last time you spoke to your mother?"

Seth felt heat rising up the back of his neck. "My parents got it in their heads that they wanted to sell the house and get an RV so they could do some traveling. They went to Florida for Christmas."

"The body of the woman has already been identified as possibly being Miriam Sinclair."

"Who identified her?" Seth asked, anger overcoming him.

"Kyle Sinclair—Graber".

"Kyle?" he asked. "Since when is Graber his last name, and what does Kyle have to do with any of this?"

"Do you know him?" the officer asked.

"He's my cousin. At least I think he is."

The officer flashed him a sympathetic look. "The body was found on his father's property."

Seth shook his head. "None of this makes any sense," he said. "Kyle's dad is dead."

The officer shook his head. "Not according to my notes. It says here, we arrested Kyle's dad as a possible suspect."

"Are we talking about the same Kyle?" Seth asked.

"We arrested a man named—just a minute, let me be certain," the officer said, pausing to look at his notes again. "Yes, we arrested Zeb Yoder, Kyle Graber's father."

Seth smirked. "That solves your whole problem right there!" he said. "The Kyle I know is a Sinclair, just like me, and his father's name was Bruce. That man sounds Amish. My cousin is anything *but* Amish."

"Not according to the notes," the officer said. "But if you come with me to the station and fill in some of the gaps, I'm sure we can sort all of this out. If you're unable to identify the body, then you won't be needed any further."

"I can tell you right now you're wasting your time. My parents are in Florida!"

Chapter 7

Seth found it hard to breathe as he followed the officer down a long, lonesome corridor. When they approached the morgue, one of the fluorescent bulbs buzzed and flickered, setting his teeth on edge.

The darkness that shrouded him weighed down his conscience.

If only he'd been able to convince his father to use the cell phone he'd presented them with when they'd gone off on their adventure. The stubborn man had resisted instruction, and had even managed to convince his son they were better off without the use of the modern device.

If only he'd insisted.

Now, he paced down the eerily quiet corridor, and the only question that plagued him was; where was his father now if his mother was truly lying dead behind the cold door of the morgue?

He knew he hadn't been the best son that two parents could have, but he always thought they were proud of him. He'd shamed his parents with the trouble he'd gotten himself into; trouble that had become all too common-place in recent years.

He rubbed at his eyes.

They wouldn't stop twitching.

His hands shook at his sides, as he lifted a shaky limb to wipe the sweat from his brow. Blowing out a worrisome breath, the buzzing of the florescent bulbs overhead filled him with an irritation he couldn't rid himself of.

The whole ride over, he'd tried to reach his sisters, but it was already late when he'd first encountered the police officer. And now, that encounter seemed so far away and so insignificant compared to what he was about to face.

He'd never attended a funeral before, let alone been close to a dead body. The possibility of the woman being his own mother made him sick to his stomach, and his knees felt a bit wobbly.

The door to the morgue opened with a click that echoed through the empty corridor. He flinched at the sound that reverberated against his eardrums like a bolt of lightning, sending a current of electricity through his veins until it reached his brain with a stabbing pain. There, it brought him instant grief he could hold in no longer.

His throat swelled and his breath hitched as he followed the officer into the brightly lit room that smelled of formaldehyde. Bile rose up in his throat, and he feared he might vomit, but he was determined to stay strong.

It wasn't his mother that was dead. They'd made a mistake—Kyle had made a mistake.

He was stronger than this. He'd take a look at the body, and he'd laugh it off when it was over, because that's who he was. He wasn't a weak little boy—he was a man, and men didn't break down.

Get ahold of yourself before you embarrass yourself. Tough it up! And when it's over—walk it off.

Seth allowed the officer to lead him to a stainless steel slab that had been pulled from a wall filled with latched doors—like a big freezer. A body draped in a sheet lay on that slab, a pair of dainty feet poking out, a manila tag hanging from one toe. He shuddered and paused. This was like watching a TV show—except it was happening to him!

This was real.

He stopped.

He wasn't up for seeing a dead body. On the off-chance it *was* his mother lying there, he didn't want to know.

"Look," he said with a shaky voice. "I'm not the guy to do this. That isn't my mother. You need to get her family to identify her, and that ain't me!"

"I'm not going to force you, Son, but she's going to remain a *Jane Doe* until we can get a positive identification on her, and that could take months of searching through missing person files. It might even be impossible if there's no record of her because she's Amish."

"Amish!" Seth said with a raised voice. "My mother wasn't Amish! Now I *know* you've got the wrong guy."

Seth stormed out of the morgue and came face-to-face with Kyle. He paused, not saying a word.

"I'm sorry," Kyle offered. "I didn't want you to find out this way!"

Chapter 8

Zeb sat in the cold room with the two-way mirror staring straight ahead. He knew why he was there, but he had nothing to say to these *Englishers*. They had no idea how hard he'd worked to keep the sins of his past hidden, hoping that one day he'd be welcomed back into the community he'd felt lost without. They didn't care about him or what he needed. They'd interrupted his one chance at seeking the forgiveness he desperately needed, and now he would be forever banned. There would be no more chances, and no peace for him.

"Let me begin by informing you that we found your DNA on the body, but we don't believe you killed her," the detective said to Zeb. "I think you already know we found someone else's DNA on her body too. Most of it was under her fingernails—probably from scratching the person who strangled her. I think you know who did this. We have reason to believe you were present at the scene of the crime, and possibly helped to bury her body in your back yard!"

He'd been read his rights. He knew he had the right to keep silent, and he intended to exercise that right.

"You can tell us the truth and help us catch the person who killed her, or you might end up having to stand trial alone, and face murder charges."

His threats meant nothing to Zeb. He no longer cared what happened to him. The only thing that mattered to him was hearing the words he longed to hear from the Bishop—the words of forgiveness the man never got a chance to speak to him. Zeb desperately needed those words in order to have peace. His very soul depended on them.

"We've done the autopsy, but we still don't have a positive ID on the body. Perhaps you want to tell us who she is so we can contact her family."

Zeb looked beyond the officer and stared at the dark, mirrored wall, wondering who was watching him from behind the glass.

He remained silent.

"Have it your way, Mr. Yoder," the officer warned. "Just understand the more you're able to tell us, the easier things will go for you. Especially since we have a new report of another grave with the wrong woman lying in it—a woman we understand you may have poisoned."

Zeb thought of his beloved Rose. She'd betrayed him—threatened to tell the Bishop and their son of his infidelity and indiscretions. He knew it was only a matter of time before she drank the tea he'd brought her. He'd read in the newspaper they'd not only mistaken her body to be that of his mistress, Selma, but they'd also ruled her death as accidental. The blow to her head when she'd hit the glass table had been the cause of death on record. He knew better. He knew she'd fallen because of the tea. At the time, it had been the perfect crime of passion, but now, it seemed that Selma had spoken out, and there would be no explanation that would keep suspicion from linking him to the crime.

Chapter 9

Seth pushed past his cousin, not willing to entertain his foolish notions. Not only did he look ridiculous, but he wasn't about to engage in a confrontation with him right now. He was angry, there was no doubt about that, but he had some things to sort out, and his foolish cousin would only be in his way.

"Wait a minute Seth," Kyle said, calling after him as he followed closely on his heels. "I want to talk to you about this."

"I have nothing to say to you, *Cousin,*" he said angrily over his shoulder. "We have absolutely nothing to talk about!"

"What about your mother?" Kyle started to ask.

Seth turned on his heels and leered at Kyle. "That woman in that morgue is *not* my mother!" he said through gritted teeth. "And I don't appreciate this game you're playing with me."

"I'm not playing any game," Kyle pleaded with him. "This is serious."

Seth turned around and stopped suddenly, his breath coming out in ragged blows. "If you're not playing games with me," he said. "Then why are you dressed like an Amish man? Is this some sort of sick, April Fool's joke? You're celebrating a little early for that, don't you think?"

"I can assure you, Cousin, this is no joke!"

"Not a joke, huh? Then why did I have a police officer telling me that your *father*," he said, holding up his fingers to make air-quotes. "Is an Amish man?"

Kyle hung his head and looked down at the freshly-buffed square tiles of the floor, and blew out a heavy sigh. "It's a very long story, and I didn't want you to hear about all of this—not now—not like this. I was trying to find you so I could break the news to you gently."

"What news, Kyle? What news could you possibly have for me? That you decided to be Amish? That you like playing tricks on people and making them think their mother is dead? Or do you just get pure joy from ticking me off?"

"I don't even know what to tell you first," he said, discouragement clouding his thoughts. "Honestly, I just found out that my mother was really Amish."

"And how did you come to such an idiotic conclusion, *Cousin?* And I use that term lightly!"

"Because my mother has been alive all this time," he began.

"And mine isn't?" Seth interrupted, his jaw clenched.

"I don't know," Kyle said quietly. "I have a lot to tell you, but things are a bit of a mess right now."

Seth threw his head back and chuckled angrily.

"Such as you being Amish, and your mother being alive? I went to your mother's funeral with you, do you remember?" he said, wagging his finger at Kyle. "I saw her body in the casket with my own eyes."

"I did too," Kyle said, swallowing a lump in his throat, remembering how he'd felt that day. "It turns out it was her sister that died, and we mistook her for my mother, but that doesn't change the fact that you need to see if that woman in there is *your* mother."

"Let's not talk about that right now! Let's talk about you and this Amish get-up," he said, flicking Kyle's black hat with the back of his hand.

"This is all because I'm embracing my mother's Amish heritage. That, and I'm in love with an Amish girl. But none of that is important right now. What's important, is *your* mother."

"*My* mother is in Florida right now with my father, and they're both alive and well. My mother is not that woman lying on that cold slab wearing a toe tag!"

"Did you even look at her?" Kyle dared to ask.

"Why would I look at the dead body of a woman I don't know?" he said, as he began to walk away. "Let her family take care of her!"

"But *we* are her family," Kyle said around the lump in his throat. "Don't you want to know what happened to her?"

Seth bit back tears. "It's not my problem what happened to that woman! And for the record, *you* are not my family—especially if you're Amish!"

"But what about your mother?" Kyle argued.

"If that's my mother in there, maybe I don't want to know. But I do want to know more about the man who killed that woman. I hear it was your *father*. Funny, but did your father come back from the dead too?"

"No, actually," he said with downcast eyes. "It just so happens, I found out recently that my father is also an Amish man."

"The same one who killed that woman in there?" Seth accused.

Kyle sighed. "Quite possibly," he said, feeling embarrassed. "I wanted to tell you everything, but so much has happened recently that I just haven't had time to contact you. But I was trying to find you to tell you this news."

"Again, Cousin," Seth said coldly. "What news could you possibly have for me? If it has anything to do with that dead woman lying in there, I don't want to hear it."

"Seth, I'm sorry," Kyle pleaded with him. "I didn't want to hear it when I found out my own mother was gone, but it turns out she wasn't the one that had died. It's a long, sordid story, and I don't have time to go into that now. I'll tell you all about it later. Right now, that woman in there deserves to be identified."

"Not by me!" Seth said angrily.

"Not even if it turns out she's your mother?" Kyle asked.

Seth narrowed his gaze on his cousin.

"Especially if she's my mother!"

Chapter 10

Seth stood outside the morgue and lit his cigarette, closing his eyes and inhaling deeply, holding it there for a moment to calm his nerves. Kyle exited the building, following closely on Seth's heels. He'd allowed him to ride down the elevator alone, hoping it would give him a moment to calm down, but now he needed to talk to him and try to reason with him.

"What was that all about, Cousin?" Kyle asked when he caught up with Seth.

"I don't know," he replied angrily. "All I do know, is that we're not cousins!"

"You've known me your whole life," Kyle argued. "I might call you friend in addition to *cousin,* but we're as polar opposite as two guys can be. We always have been, but that doesn't make us any less family."

"I think it's finally obvious you and I are *not* family," he said, letting his gaze travel over Kyle's attire.

Kyle shook his head with disgust. "I've known you my whole entire life, Seth, and I'd have to say that walking out of that morgue before making sure that woman was not your mother, was the most selfish thing you've ever done."

"Kyle, you look ridiculous. Really, you're embarrassing yourself."

"Never mind about me; we're talking about *you* right now."

"No, Cousin, we're talking about you, and how ridiculous you are," Seth said with an angry chuckle. "I can't even take you seriously in that Amish get-up!"

"I might look ridiculous to you, but for the first time in my life, I know who I am, and I'm embracing it. My mother hid from me and the world, who she was. She was Amish, and there's no shame in that."

"And what of your new *father*? He's a murderer, and he's Amish. Are you proud of the heritage that a murderer passed down to you?"

"I'm not responsible for his sins. There are bad people all over the world, and being Amish doesn't make you immune to sin. But it's not up to us if he's forgiven; his judgment will come from God, not from us. I'll admit it doesn't sit well with me to have a blood relative who's in this kind of trouble, but in all fairness, you've been quite troublesome yourself for a while now, and I still care what happens to you."

Seth took an aggressive step toward Kyle and gritted his teeth. "You dare compare my harmless mischief to the crimes of murder?"

"No one said anything about comparing you, but a sin is a sin, no matter how big or small."

"So now you're calling me a sinner, Cousin?"

"We're all sinners, but each of us is equally entitled to the forgiveness that God offers, no matter how big or small our sins are."

"Don't preach to me, Cousin," Seth said bitterly. "Until you can convince me that you're perfect, you've got no room to talk."

"I *don't* have any room to talk, but the difference between you and me is that I'm willing to admit I'm a sinner. But we're getting off track. Whether we're blood relative or not; in my heart, you'll always be my cousin. But above all, you're my friend, and I loved your mother as my aunt. I, for one, want to know what happened to her. I hope you're with me on that, because I'd hate to think I have to deal with this all alone, just because you want to bail every time things get a little too uncomfortable for you. When you're part of a family, you do whatever it takes for those you love. In family, there's no room for selfishness of any kind. If it affects you, it affects me. I've got your back, but I hope you've got mine if things get rough."

Seth rolled his eyes. "You say that now, but where were you all this time I've needed you. I'm not sure if you realize it, but I've been without a family life for quite some time."

"Honestly, Seth, you really have only yourself to blame. I've been here all along, and you've made the choice to hang out with people who are walking the thin line of the law. I imagine you're walking that fine line yourself a little, or you wouldn't have gotten here the way you did," he said, gesturing to the building where the woman was waiting to be identified.

Seth pulled his collar up to keep out the snow.

"What are you talking about?"

"I'm talking about the police officer who brought you here. I got a phone call explaining to me that you almost got carted off to jail, but instead, he brought you here on my insistence."

"So now I should be grateful to you for doing me a favor?"

Kyle gestured to the dark sky against the soft glow of the lamps that illuminated the light snow flurries.

"You may not be aware of the time, Seth, but it's the middle of the night! I wouldn't be here, except I made the officers who unearthed that woman's body promise me that if they found you or your sisters, or Uncle Jack, that they were to call me— day or night. I was *that* worried my family would have to go through this alone. I wanted to be here to explain the best I could about this because I didn't want any of you to have to hear it from strangers."

Seth scoffed. "In case you hadn't already noticed, we *are* strangers. Go back to your perfect, Amish world where people get away with murder, and leave me alone. I'm going home to get some sleep."

"No one is getting away with anything, Seth. He's been arrested, and he'll stand trial the same as anyone else, but the outcome will be up to the justice system, not you or me."

"What about—*her?*" Seth asked. "Where was her justice?"

"You're right, there was *no* justice for her, but she certainly has the right to be identified."

"Let's get something straight, *Cousin.* The *only* reason I'm here is so I could avoid jail. That officer caught up with me a second time, and I had to cooperate with him, or get myself arrested. So, I agreed to come look at a dead body. Turns out, my stomach is weaker than I thought it was, and I couldn't go through with it. I think I'd rather go to jail than to go in there and face the possibility of that dead woman being my mother."

Seth bit his lower lip and turned away from Kyle to keep him from seeing the emotion that overcame him. He would not break down in front of the *Golden Boy.*

Everything had always come easy for Kyle. From school, to making friends—the right kind of friends. Kyle had a way about him that made him always rise to the top, no matter what. He was smart in a way that Seth couldn't grasp. He was everything opposite from Seth. He, himself, was by no means unintelligent, but he seemed to use his smarts for the wrong things—things that seemed to bring him nothing but trouble. He was certain Kyle had never been in the slightest of trouble.

"You don't have to go in there alone," Kyle offered. "I'll be right there with you. And no matter which way it turns out, I'll be here for you."

"We've come a long way from becoming *blood brothers* when we were kids, Kyle."

He nodded. "It's true; we aren't boys anymore, but the pact I made with you still remains. We may not be cousins, but I'll always honor that blood brother pact I made with you when we were just kids."

Seth nodded slowly and agreed to go with Kyle back into the building. The only thing that would drive him back to the elevator was remembering the last words he'd spoken to his mother. He'd made a promise to her the day she and his dad had left for Florida.

He'd promised to straighten out his life, and he'd let her down.

Chapter 11

Seth took one last drag of a cigarette before
snuffing it out with the toe of his boot. He paused,
wondering if there was a way to avoid what he
was about to do but nothing came to him. His
mind was too cluttered with fear of the possibility
that his mother was dead. Kyle would not let him
out of his obligation no matter how much he
protested. Deep down, he knew he owed his
mother that much and more, but that didn't make it
any easier.

Seth counted the floor tiles as he walked over each one along the long cold corridor that led to the morgue. He knew if he didn't keep his mind occupied on something that mattered very little, he feared he might go mad just from the terror that he felt deep within his gut. The clack of his boots kept time with Kyle's, the sound echoing like wild horses thundering across wide-open country.

He tried to reason with himself that Kyle had mistaken the woman's identity, and he'd hear from his parents any day now. He'd make the changes he'd promised his mother, and his family would be together again the way they were when he was a young boy.

His mind flashed to the last Christmas they'd spent together, and the strain of his condescending sisters and their perfect lives being shoved down his throat. He'd been glad his parents had packed up and left on their cross-country trip. It had meant he no longer had to be accountable for his actions—despite the promise he'd made to his mother to change his ways.

There would be no more empty promises over a piece of her molasses pie that he loved so much. What was it she'd called that pie?

Shoo-fly pie.

They'd come to the end of the corridor, and the end of Seth's aimless thoughts. There was no turning back now.

Kyle flashed him a look of compassion as he pushed open the heavy door to the morgue, where the coroner was closing the woman's body back into the freezer. Glancing back at them, he pulled the drawer back open and pulled back the sheet without saying a word to either of them. He took a step back and busied himself in the corner as Kyle moved further into the room, Seth in his shadow.

Kyle glanced over his shoulder at his cousin, who seemed to be cowering near the door. His look of disappointment sent his cousin across the room toward the body on the slab.

There, he stood frozen, just like the body.

Seth stared with unseeing eyes at the woman on the slab. He didn't dare feel; didn't dare think, lest he would break down. He'd been brought up to be strong; he was taught that only girls and the weak cry. Swallowing down the lump that formed in his throat, he clenched his jaw against the emotion that threatened to bring tears; tears that would show weakness.

Anger filled him as his gaze traveled to the look of unrest on her decayed face. He'd been told that her body had been mostly preserved due to the cold weather conditions at the time of her burial. Regardless, he'd know his mother, and this woman was certainly her, but how?

"My father," Seth managed quietly without turning away from her. "Has anyone told him yet, or has he known all this time and didn't tell me? Where could he be all this time? Why isn't he here?"

"The police are following a lead to an address I found," Kyle said. "It was from a post office in Florida, but the letter was post-marked Pigeon Hollow."

"What sort of letter?"

"It was a letter from your parents to your sister, and it claimed they'd arrived in Florida, but it was post-marked here. Like I said, it doesn't make any sense."

Seth stared at his mother's face. Her hair was smoothed back, and lacked the luster it once had. Her skin was grey, and looked almost rubbery—like the dolphins at the aquarium.

"I'd say she's proof they didn't make it out of the county, and they certainly never made it to Florida."

Kyle swallowed hard the lump in his throat at the realization of Seth's confirmation.

The coroner stepped forward. "Can you confirm her identity?"

He nodded coldly as he took in a deep breath and blew it out slowly, trying to control his emotions.

Kyle put a hand on his shoulder. "Do you need a moment?"

He shook his head slightly. "There isn't anything I can do for her here."

"I have some paperwork I'll need you to fill out," he said with a clinical sort of automation.

Kyle supposed the man had become immune to the emotions of the loved-ones who would have to do the identifying. Still, his lack of compassion was a little unnerving.

"Where's that letter?" Seth asked. "I need to see if it's my mother's handwriting on it."

Chapter 12

Kyle stared out the kitchen window, washing his hands for dinner. He turned back to look at Caleb, who was putting a pot of stew on the table for his wife.

"Hey," he said. "There's a light on at the old man's house."

Caleb crossed the room and stood at the window with his brother. He turned to Kyle, his face flushed. "You don't suppose he's holding someone else hostage over there, do you?" He asked half-jokingly.

Kyle reflected for a moment on the terror his mother had suffered at the hands of Zeb Yoder, and his heart beat hard against his chest wall.

"Well, I think we can pretty much rule out the old man since he's in jail, but I had no idea he had electricity in the house."

"He doesn't," Caleb said matter-of-factly. "Which means, whoever is in there probably flipped on the switch to the gas lights without knowing they were gas."

"Do you think it could be a prowler? Maybe we should go check it out." Kyle said.

Caleb looked at Amelia, and she shooed him with her hand. "Go ahead," she said before he asked. "I'll hold dinner for you. I know if you don't go check it out, you'll be getting up every five minutes and looking out the window out of curiosity."

Caleb smiled and kissed his wife on the cheek.

"We won't be long, I promise."

The two men put on their coats and shouldered out into the cold, dark night. Once outside, Kyle unlocked the doors to his truck and they hopped in, both shivering. After starting the engine, Kyle reached under the seat and pulled out a black box and set it on the middle armrest.

Before Caleb could ask what was in the box, Kyle opened it and pulled out a large handgun. He checked the chamber and then loaded the clip. He put it back in the box without a word.

"You really think we need a gun to go over there?" Caleb asked him.

"Yes, brother, I do think I need a gun to go over there. After all the dead bodies and hostages that have turned up, I think we need to start protecting ourselves. There's no reason for anyone to be over at the old man's house, and I don't plan on being ambushed."

Caleb agreed he had a point, but having a gun in the mix made him feel a little uneasy. Had it really come to this?

They drove the short distance in silence, the tension thick between them. When he reached the driveway, he turned off his headlights and rolled up the driveway slowly. When they reached the barn, he shut off the engine and they opened the doors quietly. Kyle stuffed the gun in the back of his pants and pulled his coat over it as they walked carefully toward the house, the snow crunching beneath their boots.

As they approached the house, Caleb realized they hadn't discussed what they planned on doing if they encountered the intruder.

Kyle crept under the kitchen window where the lights were on, ducking close to the house as he slid in next to the frame. He motioned for Caleb to stick close to the house so he wouldn't be seen.

Then he pulled the gun out from the back of his pants and peered up into the window.

The kitchen was empty.

His heart did a flip-flop behind his ribcage, anticipation raising the hair on the back of his neck.

"Anyone in there?" Caleb whispered.

Kyle shook his head, and then listened to a noise that seemed to be coming from the next room in the house.

The lights went on in the living room, and Kyle advanced to that window to get a better look.

As he peered inside, he let out his breath and lowered his gun, shaking his head.

"I don't believe it," he said, walking toward the front porch.

"What?" Caleb called after him in a loud whisper. "Who's in there?"

Kyle was already on the porch, fast approaching the door, when he suddenly burst through it.

The dark-haired man dropped the stack of papers he was holding, and looked up at Kyle and Caleb as they entered the house.

"What are you doing here?" Kyle demanded.

"Are you planning on shooting me, Cousin?" Seth asked.

Kyle furrowed his brow as he stuffed the gun in the back of his pants. "Never mind that! I want to know what you're doing here."

Caleb got between the two of them. "I'd like it if someone would explain to *me* what's going on here. You know him?" he asked his brother.

"He's sort of my cousin."

Caleb nodded. He'd heard the story of the Sinclair family, and how they'd taken Kyle in when he and his mom were having problems.

He extended his hand politely. "You must be Seth; I'm Caleb Yoder."

Seth's lips formed a thin line. "Yoder?" he said through gritted teeth. "You're kin to this murderer too?"

Caleb held his hands up and shook his head. "Not by choice—no more than Kyle."

"That makes you both just as accountable for what happened to my mother—just by your association with this murderer."

"That's not fair!" Kyle said, raising his voice. "We didn't do it. We were just as surprised as you were!"

"You still haven't answered my question," Kyle continued. "What are you doing here?"

Seth blew out a sigh and motioned to the mess he'd made of the old man's house. "I'm looking for clues."

"Maybe you should let the authorities handle the investigation," Caleb advised him.

Seth took an aggressive step toward him. "What have they done to help any of the old man's victims so far?"

Caleb had to agree he had a point, but he didn't like the idea of Seth snooping around, and perhaps messing with evidence that could be used in the investigation.

"How'd you get in here, anyway?"

"The same way you just did—through the door!"

"Did you break in?" Caleb grilled him.

"No! The door was unlocked."

Caleb thought back to the Bishop's visit, and realized they had been so wrapped up in unearthing the body of the Amish woman, they had probably left the door unlocked.

"Say, how do you explain the Amish clothing she was wearing when—you know…" Caleb stammered.

"When your father murdered her?" Seth accused. "Maybe he has some strange fetish with Amish women, and he made her wear the clothes before he did the deed!"

"You're not Amish?" Caleb asked.

"No!" Seth said with a chuckle. "You can't see that just by looking at me?"

Caleb shrugged. "I thought perhaps your mother might have been. Kyle didn't know his mom was Amish until recently."

Seth leered at him. "Let me just stop you right there. My mother wasn't Amish, and there was no deep dark secret involved with her death. I think your old man just likes to...*hurt women!"*

"I'm not going to argue with you there, but don't lump us in with him," Kyle said. "We're just as invested in finding out what happened as you are."

"No you're not!" he accused his cousin. "Your mother is alive!"

"Mine isn't," Caleb stepped in. "He poisoned *my* mother!"

Seth's look softened a little, and he lowered his gaze. "I didn't know that."

"Now that you do, perhaps we can all work together."

"Why don't you come back to the house with us and have a little dinner," Kyle offered.

Seth looked around at the mess he'd made. "I am a little hungry."

"It's settled then," Caleb said. "My wife made enough beef stew and biscuits to feed an army, and she'll be happy to set another place for you."

He nodded and grabbed his coat.

"You want to get the lights?" Caleb asked.

Seth shook his head. "I plan on coming back after we eat!"

"I'm not so sure that's a good idea," Kyle said.

"Look here, Cousin; I plan on camping out here until I find something solid that explains why the old man did what he did!"

"I don't think anyone but him knows why he's done the things he's done," Caleb said soberly.

"I'm not sure if the old man can do anything about you being here, but…"

Seth held up a hand to interrupt him. "The old man is never going to know. He's in jail, right?"

"Yeah, but what about the police? What if they think you're interfering with their investigation?"

He smirked. "They don't have a choice!"

Chapter 13

Seth tossed his cigarette out the car window as he turned into the long drive that led to the Amish farmhouse. He'd followed Kyle back to Caleb's home, who had turned out to be his half-brother. His cousin's life, it would seem, had become even more complicated than his own, if that was possible. He was numb, and needed some time to think. He certainly wasn't in the mood for socializing, but his growling stomach betrayed his need for solitude.

His sisters had turned him away the last few times he'd spoken to them, and so he'd decided to allow the authorities to break the news to them. He knew it was the coward's way out, but he just couldn't face them after the last conversation he'd had with them.

They'd both complained he wasn't a good influence on his young nephews and nieces. They were right, and he wondered if things would be more estranged between them once they learned the news of their mother. He felt guilty for not being there when the news was broken to them, but he feared he wouldn't be well received.

Anger raged inside him at the thought of the anguish his mother had suffered at the hands of the man who'd killed her. And now, he was about to break bread with the descendants of the murderer. How could he possibly explain his association with this family to his sisters? It would only perpetuate their distrust for him. They likely wouldn't accept Kyle's connection to the man, nor his close relationship with the son who'd grown up with the murderer.

Things were becoming more complicated by the minute, and he wasn't sure he was ready for all of this acceptance just yet. He couldn't look the other way and become friends with Caleb, and he certainly couldn't account for his cousin's blindness to the situation.

He pulled his car in behind Kyle's truck, wondering if he'd be able to desensitize himself to the death of his mother long enough to be cordial during dinner. He couldn't help but feel that he'd traded his loyalty to his mother for a home-cooked meal.

Suddenly feeling sick in his gut, he took a deep breath of the damp, wintry air and blew it out slowly. He hoped it would make him feel better, but it didn't. He was certain his mother would be rolling over in her grave—that is, if she was in a proper one yet.

He worried about the arrangements, even though he knew his sisters would take over the situation and handle things *their way.* He wasn't looking forward to facing his family at the funeral, especially since he'd not done as he'd promised and set his life on the straight-and-narrow path.

It was too late for all of that anyway. He'd failed to make his mother proud in her last days on this earth, and it weighed heavily on his heart.

He exited his car and pulled out a cigarette, flicking his Zippo to light it, and suddenly changed his mind, realizing he no longer had the stomach for it.

Stuffing the cigarette back in the box, and the lighter in his pocket, he followed his cousin into Caleb's house, the wonderful aroma of food momentarily clouding over the feeling of unrest that plagued him.

As they entered in through the kitchen, introductions were made, and Seth robotically greeted each of the women with feigned interest.

All, except for one—Kyle's mother.

He was more than a little interested in how she managed to escape the old man's captivity, and come out of it alive. Especially since his own mother had failed to do so.

Seth intended to grill her for information about the old man. He wanted to know all he could about the man, and what made him tick. He would study the man's character through his victim's eyes if need-be in order to prove his guilt for the crime.

Though he wasn't wild about the idea of getting into the mind of a murderer, he knew that learning his character traits would help solve what happened. After all, he'd watched enough of those forensic shows that he figured he was smart enough to figure it all out.

How hard could it be?

Chapter 14

"Seth, you can't be serious about staying at the old man's house, could you?" Kyle asked.

"I was really hoping your mom could give me some information I could use to figure out why this happened, but all she did was confuse me by telling me how much she missed me, and what good of friends she and my mother were when they were young," he complained. "So, yes! I'm absolutely going to stay at his house. I figure he owes me that much."

"Are you homeless?" Kyle caught him off-guard with the remark.

He shifted his weight from one foot to the other, and looked off in the distance.

"Not exactly. I lost my condo in a poker game, and I've been living in the rat-infested loft of the guy who won it. I've been there for the last two weeks," he admitted. "But as soon as Frankie sets up the big game for me on Saturday, I'll get my condo back from that hustler!"

"Isn't that what *you've* become? A hustler?"

"Don't judge me, Amish boy!"

"I personally don't care if you stay there, but I can't answer for Caleb."

"How does it feel to find out after all these years that your old man is a murderer?" Seth accused.

"What he's done has nothing to do with me—any more than my choices in life would affect him!"

"Whatever," Seth grumbled.

"Just be careful," Kyle warned his cousin. "I'm not sure how well it would go over with the detective if you mess up his investigation."

"He isn't doing his job fast enough for me!" he said snuffing out the cigarette he'd taken only one drag from.

"I'll come over there tomorrow afternoon and see if you've come up with anything. I think I'm going to sleep in a little tomorrow. This stress has caused me to lose a lot of sleep. You could stand to get some yourself. Don't stay awake all night."

"I'm a grown man, Cousin," he growled. "I think I can decide for myself when I need sleep."

With that, he hopped in his BMW and backed down the driveway. He had nothing more to say to his overbearing cousin. His only thoughts were of his mother, and finding out exactly what happened to her.

Within minutes, he'd pulled into the driveway of the Yoder farm, realizing the lights were off. Had Kyle gone behind him and turned out the lights? Strangely, he couldn't' remember. The only thing he could remember was the remark about turning them off, but now he couldn't be sure if they were on or off when they'd left the house.

He grabbed a flashlight from the trunk and proceeded into the house. If, for some reason, the gas lights weren't working, he'd have to locate the lanterns he'd seen scattered around the place earlier.

Once on the porch, he stomped the snow off his boots and went inside, trying the light switch.

Nothing.

He flicked the switch of his flashlight, but the batteries were low, and only a dim light glowed from the end. He tapped the end of it, knowing sometimes it would make the bulb brighter, but this time it failed him.

The familiar, metallic click of a pump-action shotgun from the other side of the room stopped him dead in his tracks. He raised the short beam of the flashlight with a shaky hand, aiming it on an old man with a long, white beard.

"You're trespassing!" the old man barked.

"Who are you?" Seth asked, backing toward the door.

The man pointed the gun at him. "I should be asking you that question since this is my *haus,* and you're trespassing!"

Seth could feel the blood draining from his head. He was dizzy, and breathing was suddenly difficult for him.

"You killed my mother!" Seth accused, as he charged toward the old man, adrenaline making him fearless of the danger.

With one quick motion, Zeb jerked the gun to the left and shot toward the wall, and Seth felt a sting penetrating the flesh of his shoulder. His flashlight hit the floor, and the narrow beam went dark.

"Are you completely crazy, Old Man?" Seth shouted. "You shot me!"

The old man chuckled. "I just winged you with a stray pellet. Next time it'll be a gut-shot. Now get back real slow, and keep your hands where I can see them while you explain to me why you're trespassing on my property!"

"Why don't you tell me how you escaped from jail!" Seth demanded.

"They can't hold a man on suspicion," Zeb said, striking a match and lighting a lantern.

"Suspicion?" Seth accused. "You're a murderer!"

"They don't have any proof," he said with a chuckle. "All they have is hearsay!"

"What about Kyle's mom? She can testify to you kidnapping her!"

"She isn't going to press any charges against me!"

"How can you be so sure of that?" he asked, gazing around the room for anything he could use to overpower the man with the gun pointed at him.

"Amish ways are forgiveness," he said, calmly.

"Well, I don't forgive you for murdering my mother; I'll press charges against you!"

"You must be Seth," Zeb said casually. "And you're wrong. I didn't kill your mother, her husband did!"

Chapter 15

"You're insane! My father wouldn't do such a thing!"

"Your father?" Zeb asked casually. "Now that's where you're wrong."

Seth's heart sped up, but he couldn't resist asking the question. "What am I wrong about?"

"Jack Sinclair isn't your father!"

"Yeah? Who do you suppose is my father? You?"

Zeb chuckled. "Now you're catching on, boy!"

"You're a liar!" he shouted. "My mother was in love with my father, and she wouldn't take up with the likes of you!"

Zeb looked him in the eye, his expression twinkling with delight over Seth's reaction to the news. "We were young then, and she was acquainted with Jack at the time. As a matter of fact, she married him only two short weeks after spending the night with me in my parent's barn."

Seth could feel his torso weakening, his knees wobbling at the very thought of it. He clutched his middle, wondering if he would lose his dinner. He cringed as he set his gaze upon the old man.

It wasn't true. It couldn't be.

Sweat formed on his brow, the sting of the shotgun pellet fading in comparison to the words the old man spoke. Kyle had described the same situation with the old man. He'd said the same words to him, but why would he be saying them now?

It was absurd to even think about.

Still, it had turned out to be the truth for Kyle.

Unable to stand any longer on his wobbly legs, Seth dropped to his knees, tunnel vision threatening a total blackout.

His thoughts reeled.

Being the son of a murderer was not something he could live with. Was his relation to the old man the reason behind his rebellious streak that Jack could never seem to tame?

"Did my father—*Jack,* know about—what you're saying?"

"Your mother had deceived him all those years," the old man reflected. "I agreed to keep her confidence as long as she came to *visit* me on a regular basis."

Seth could feel the bile rising in his throat at the old man's statement.

"My mother wouldn't have betrayed my father like that."

"The day she died, she came to see me. She came to tell me goodbye; that she was leaving for

Florida with her husband. Naturally, I couldn't let her go."

"So you killed her!" Seth accused weakly.

"I loved her; I wouldn't kill her."

"You didn't love her! You might have sewed some wild oats with her when the two of you were young, but you did *not love* her!"

Zeb smiled. "*Jah,* the days during our *rumspringa* were quite joyful."

Seth had only just found out what that term meant at dinner, having discussed the old man being Kyle's father.

And now he was claiming to be Seth's father!

That would make me Amish—and a brother to Kyle and Caleb, he thought.

"Those days might have been joyful for you— sewing your wild oats all over the community, but if it was so great for the young girls you took advantage of, they would have stayed with you instead of marrying other men."

"Well, I can't deny that Rose was my true love."

"Isn't she Caleb's mother? The one you poisoned?"

"She was going to expose my sins to the Bishop!"

Seth held a hand over his mouth, sure he was going to vomit.

"So you killed her to keep her quiet?"

"I merely banned her from my presence, and that of Caleb. She knew there was poison in the tea. I told her! It's not my fault she chose to drink it."

"Why don't we get back to *my mother,* and how you murdered her!"

Zeb raised the gun angrily. "I already told you, boy; I didn't kill your mother. Jack killed her."

A sudden feeling of dread made him sweat.

"Why do I get the feeling you know where my father is? The police can't find him, but I'd be willing to bet you know."

The old man smirked. "Your mother told me you were a betting man. What do you suppose the odds are that Jack is here?"

"I'd say pretty high," Seth said. "But I get the feeling the odds of him being alive are about zero!"

"I'd say you guessed that one right!"

Seth let out a strangled cry. "Oh, you didn't?"

"That was an accident—like the shot that hit you."

"That was no accident!" he sobbed. "It was deliberate. You pulled that trigger; the gun didn't go off by accident."

Zeb turned up the lantern. "I suppose you have me on that one, boy."

"Sounds like you're admitting you killed my father deliberately, too."

"Let's get something straight, boy. I'm your father—not Jack Sinclair. And the shot I took at him was just to scare him like I did to you just now, but I was a bit groggy still from being hit on the head by him. I told you he followed her that day, and when he overheard the truth, he had a breakdown and came at me with a shovel, ironically."

Seth found it hard to breathe. "What do you mean, *ironically?*"

"Because it's the same shovel I used to bury him," Zeb said gruffly.

Chapter 16

Seth remained doubled over. He was certainly exposing his weakness to the old man.

He stood and crossed the room, aiming the gun at Seth. "Get up!" Zeb ordered him. "Now that you're here, you're going to help me move Jack's body. If they find his grave, they'll take me back to jail, and I'm not going to let that happen."

Seth rose to his feet, contemplating whether or not to charge toward the old man. He knew the likelihood of him getting shot was pretty high, but he had no intention of helping him cover up murder. Now he understood what his mother meant all those times she tried to get him to change his ways. It all made sense; she didn't want him turning out like the man who shared his DNA.

Zeb ordered him out the door, and Seth remained quiet while he thought of a way out of his dilemma. His mother had instilled one good trait in him, and that was to remain silent when the situation called for it, which this one did.

If he resisted anymore, the old man would certainly shoot him. He also knew that the man was not dumb, and would know better than to let him go when he knew too much.

Seth concluded the only thing he could do was to cooperate. It was his only chance at staying alive.

They walked out the door, and Seth wondered if he could make it to his car before the shotgun went off. His shoulder still stung from the pellet lodged there, and the old man seemed like the type to shoot an unarmed man in the back.

Though he wasn't wild about digging up his father's grave, he knew he probably needed to see it for himself to believe it. He also knew, from watching cop shows on TV, that the likelihood of a killer turning on you was less if you could keep him talking. He knew it was foolish to put his trust in anything he'd ever seen on TV being true-to-life, but he had nothing else to hope for at the moment.

"Tell me what happened that night when my mother came to meet you."

"You really want to know the details of her death?"

"Yes!"

"Jack overheard our conversation and accused me of soiling your mother. He threatened to kill her so neither of us would have her," Zeb said from behind him.

They walked past his car, and he knew that even getting the old man to talk was not enough of a distraction to get away. He was certain he'd dropped his car keys on the floor when the old man had surprised him with the gun, so it was really a moot point anyway.

"You can get a shovel and a pickaxe out of the shed right there," Zeb told him. "And don't get any wise ideas about hitting me with it. I've already warned you I'll put a hole in your gut."

"You still didn't tell me how my mother died," Seth questioned him as he walked toward the shed.

Zeb stood behind him and held up the lantern so he could see to get the tools he'd need for digging.

"We got into a fight, and he hit me on the head with the shovel. When I came-to, he was choking your mother."

Seth turned sharply. "You expect me to believe that my own father strangled my mother? He loved her."

"I believe the *Englishers* called that a *crime of passion.*"

"How did my father die?"

Zeb pushed the gun between Seth's shoulder blades. "We need to get something straight, boy.

I'm your father, and you better get used to saying it."

Seth swallowed hard and clenched his jaw as he lifted the pickaxe from its hook, contemplating the risk of swinging it at the old man and missing his target.

"Okay, how did *Jack* die?"

"Like I said, when I came-to, he was hunched over her and choking her. I picked up my gun and shot toward him. I was still a little wobbly from the blow to my head and I suppose I overshot. It killed him instantly. I didn't mean to, and I only did it to defend your mother. But when I went over to her, she was already dead."

His quivering voice when he mentioned her death didn't go unnoticed by Seth.

So *that* was the old man's kryptonite!

"Why did you lie to the police and say you had no idea how she'd gotten in the casket?"

"I didn't want them to take her away," Zeb admitted.

And there it was again! His weakness—the women in his life. It was all beginning to make sense to Seth. He loved them all. He may have had his favorite—Rose, Caleb's mother, but he actually loved them all—in his own sick way.

The real question was, how many more sons had the old man fathered? How many more would turn up? Would there be casualties attached to each of them?

Seth had to put his worries aside for the time-being and concentrate on not getting shot by the unstable man. Just because his first shot had only winged him, didn't mean he wasn't capable of shooting his own flesh-and-blood. He'd threatened it, and Seth figured he'd better take the old man seriously. After all, he'd held Kyle's mother captive, and had offered Caleb's mother death as an option to betraying him.

Seth remained silent as he walked the path to the edge of the Yoder property to the site where his mother had just been unearthed.

"That's far enough," Zeb barked at him. "Dig right there, next to the other hole."

He felt a shiver run through him. It wasn't the cold, night air that was to blame. The very thought of digging up his own father's grave filled him with enough terror, he worried he might lose consciousness. The only thing that kept his faculties intact was knowing he needed to stay alert if he was to stay alive.

His nerves jangled, and his hands shook. He needed a cigarette, and he needed one badly.

Reaching into his pocket, he pulled a cigarette from the pack and flicked his lighter.

Zeb motioned to him with the gun. "You put that out or I'll shoot you right now! You should quit. It's a disgusting habit."

"So is murder," Seth said as he tossed the lit cigarette down and snuffed it out with his boot. "But I don't see you quitting that!"

"Stop talking and dig!" the old man demanded.

After setting the shovel against a nearby tree, Seth swung the pickaxe, the pain in his left shoulder escalating. He groaned against the pain, but continued to swing. Every time it came down against the frozen ground, he wanted to yell, but he knew to do that could draw attention from the farmhouse across the field. He was surprised they hadn't heard the crack from the shotgun. Being inside when he got shot, it was possible the house muffled the sound just enough they wouldn't hear it from there, and if they did, they would likely not know what it was.

As much as he could use Kyle's and Caleb's help about now—especially his cousin's gun, he didn't want to put them in danger. Was it possible he had grown that mature in the last half hour? Perhaps getting shot by a man who claimed to be kin to him was enough to wake him up and *scare him straight!*

He continued to hack at the dirt until he hit something that made a dull thud. He was less than three feet down, thinking how careless it was of the old man to dig the graves so shallow. He supposed it was due to having done the digging himself to bury the bodies in the first place.

"How did you manage to dig both of these holes without help?" Seth asked.

Zeb jerked his head up from watching him dig, and looked Seth in the eye. "Who said I had help?"

"No one! It's just that I'm sure you have at least thirty years on me, and I'm struggling."

The old man furrowed his brow. "That's because your mother never made you work an honest day in your life. That's why you're lazy and take the sinner's way and gamble."

Like you have any right to be calling me a sinner, old man!

Seth had to admit the old man had a point, but he wasn't about to agree with him because he was acting smug and judging him when he had no right to.

"I don't know what information you *think* you're going to get out of me with all these questions, but you need to be quiet!"

"Being the gambling man that I am, I don't think you're going to shoot me now, because you need me to do the digging. It's obvious you can't do the digging yourself, or you'd have done it this time too! And since I don't think my chances of coming out of this alive are that great, I'd be willing to bet my father wasn't dead when the digging was done the first time, was he? Were you holding the gun on him then?"

The old man made an aggressive move toward him with the gun. "You shut your mouth," he said through clenched teeth. "Just shut your mouth."

Seth dropped the shovel, emotion clogging his throat at the sudden realization his father had been shot in cold blood. "Oh crap! You made him dig his own grave, didn't you?"

"I said shut up!" Zeb said, stepping toward him.

Tripping on a tree branch, the old man fell to the ground and the gun fired another shot.

Chapter 17

Seth hit the ground when the gun went off, but it wasn't enough to keep the fear from overtaking him. Before he could do anything to stop it, he began to lose consciousness. The last thing he remembered was light rain hitting his face.

"Was that thunder?" Caleb asked as he looked out at the rain.

"It sounded more like a shotgun to me!" Kyle answered. "But deer season is long over. Even so, the only farm within twenty miles is the old man's."

"You think it's possible Seth is over there playing target practice?"

"No! The Seth I know wouldn't have a shotgun. He might talk real tough, but when it comes right down to it, he's the exact opposite of tough, if you know what I mean!"

"Maybe we should go check it out," Caleb said.

"In this rain? It's coming down in buckets now, and the river is already so high because of all the rain and snow we had this year, this rain is probably going to cause a washout on the road."

Caleb thought for a moment about the risk of a washout, knowing his brother was right, but he had a bad feeling. "I still think we should check it out."

Zeb lifted himself from the rapidly melting snow and went over to Seth, who'd fallen face-first into the mud. The hole was rapidly filling with water, and he'd be covered in a matter of minutes. He knew he'd drown if he left him there, and to him, it was the perfect crime. It would be ruled an accidental death, and he wouldn't have to worry about the boy knowing his secrets that could put him in jail for the rest of his days.

He wasn't about to go back to jail willingly.

A light from the road caused him to look up at a pair of headlights coming from the direction of Caleb's farm. It would be a matter of minutes before the two boys would be here, and there was not enough time to make a rational decision about Seth. By the time they found him, he'd be drowned in the mud he was lying in, but Zeb knew if he didn't leave the scene, he'd be caught and blamed for his death too.

The only place to hide was the cellar. Beneath the rubble from the barn fire, the latch still remained, and the cellar was still usable. He walked fast, slipping several times in the slush, heavy rain drenching him.

When he reached the latch, he pulled it open quickly and put his foot on the top rung of the ladder going down. It gave-way under his weight, and Zeb plummeted to the bottom of the cellar, the wind knocked from his lungs.

He struggled to draw in air, panic filling him at the pain it caused. Even in his struggle to breathe, he knew he'd broken a few ribs on impact.

He wheezed and coughed, trying to get enough air in his lungs, but it was a struggle. Forcing himself over on his other side brought some relief, but he still didn't feel he was getting enough air. He'd broken ribs before, after being thrown from a horse he was trying to break, and he knew if he propped himself up, his breathing would be easier.

He slowly and painfully reached an arm toward the center beam in the cellar and dragged himself the three feet to reach it, sliding in mud the entire way. After propping himself up, he looked up and could see rain water pouring into the cellar at an alarming rate.

He chuckled to himself, figuring that he would suffer the same fate as young Seth in this storm.

He knew the river was high, and with no barn to keep out the water, the washout would drain into the cellar, and he would probably drown.

Trapped, with broken ribs, there was no way he would get out. He couldn't help but think that it almost seemed like poetic justice to perish in the very same spot he'd held his loved-ones hostage, as he closed his eyes against the darkness that had already claimed him.

Kyle and Caleb jumped out of the truck and headed up the porch to the old man's house. They found it odd that the front door was wide open, but they hollered for Seth anyway.

Caleb tried the light switch, but nothing happened. Knowing the gas had to be turned off outside somewhere, he opted for lighting a lantern he found on the table.

Looking up at his brother, who still stood near the door waiting on the light, he pointed behind him at the hole in the wall.

Kyle went over and examined the spray of buckshot around the hole. "That's from a shotgun. We need to find Seth!"

They searched the house and found nothing.

"You don't suppose he's out there in this weather, do you?"

"His car is here and the door was open. This shotgun hole in the wall suggests he might not be alone."

Off in the distance, the sound of sirens filled their ears, and they were moving closer to the main road at the foot of the long dirt drive leading to their father's farm.

Caleb looked out at the line of police cars pulling into the driveway. "What do you suppose this is all about?"

"My guess is that the old man escaped!"

"No! How could he?"

"Not sure," Kyle said. "But I think we're about to find out what happened."

The two walked out to greet the police, but one of them stopped them abruptly.

"Stop right where you are!" he said, holding his gun out toward them. "Hand over Zebedee Yoder, and no one will get hurt."

"We don't know where he is," Kyle said. "What makes you think he's here?"

"He faked a heart attack, and when he was being transferred to the infirmary, he knocked out the guard and escaped."

"We think my cousin is here somewhere," Kyle said. "But we can't find him. Someone shot a hole in the wall inside the house with a shotgun, but there isn't any sign of the old man or Seth. Can you help us find them?"

"Let's search the grounds," one of them said.

The officers turned on their spotlights on their cars, aiming them out toward the acres of land behind the house.

"I have a million, candle-power spotlight in my truck we could use to go out and look around the property."

He was already at his truck retrieving it before anyone could protest. His only goal was to find Seth—hopefully alive.

Seth picked his head up out of the mud once more. Several minutes before, he'd watched the old man running away from him, and couldn't figure out why, but now he knew. He coughed and sputtered, trying to get the water he'd inhaled out of his lungs as he listened to the sirens coming closer. Muffled voices filled his head, but he was too weak and disoriented to yell out to them.

He tried to move, but his leg was stuck, and he was certain he'd slipped in the mud and was trapped between a thick wall of mud and his father's casket. He knew he'd hit his head pretty hard when he'd fallen, and he felt the sting most likely from an open wound on his scalp.

The voices neared him, but he wasn't certain he was dreaming them or not, and so remained in the mud-hole up to his neck now. The river water had washed in so fast, he was trapped pretty tightly against the heavy box that was still half-buried. Finding it increasingly hard to hold up his head, he gave in to the weakness and darkness that faded in and out, his head fully immersed in the muddy pool that surrounded him.

"I want you to stay here and let us handle this. We believe Mr. Yoder is armed, and he's dangerous," one of the officers warned them.

"You don't have to tell us how dangerous he is," Kyle said. "He's our father, so we know!"

"All the more reason for you to stay here and let us handle things."

"Yes, Sir," Kyle said.

Caleb turned to his brother once the officers were scattered along the property.

"Why did you tell him we'd stay here?"

"I just wanted him to leave us alone so we could go look for Seth," he answered.

"Then let's go!" Caleb urged him.

As soon as the last officer was out of site, the two grabbed Kyle's spotlight and went out to the opposite end of the property. They sloshed in the wet earth, rain still pouring down in thick sheets.

Kyle blinked away the rain, squinting against the heavy drops that blew sideways against them. "I hope we can find him out in this mess before the river rises too high."

He shone the flashlight toward the back of the property as they walked past the shed.

"The door is open!" Caleb remarked.

"I can see a shovel stuck in the ground out there, and it looks like someone might be out there too."

"Let's go!"

Terrible thoughts reeled in Kyle's head as they ran to the back of the property, trying not to slide in the slushy grass. The last thing he wanted to find back there was Seth buried where his mother used to be.

When they came upon the gravesite, they both grabbed Seth out of the muck and laid him face up.

"Is he still alive?" Caleb shouted above the rain.

Kyle collapsed to his knees at his cousin's side and swiftly pressed his head to his chest. "I can hear a heartbeat, but I can't tell if he's breathing."

Seth coughed up muddy water, and struggled to pull in air. They turned him on his side, and Kyle pounded on his back with enough force to help him cough up the rest of it so he could breathe.

He looked up at Kyle with a fading look. "My brother, you saved me."

"He's delirious!" Caleb said. "Should we call an ambulance?"

"No, he's not," Kyle said. "I think he's making perfect sense."

At that point, Kyle knew he'd had a run-in with the old man, and he'd heard the same frightening words he'd heard from him.

Seth was no longer just a blood brother from a childhood pact, he was a true blood brother who shared his same DNA.

Chapter 18

Seth tried to speak, but Kyle hushed him. It was important that he conserve his energy until the ambulance could arrive.

"The old man ran that way," Seth said weakly, barely lifting his arm to show the direction.

"He'd run into the barbed wire fence if he went that way," Kyle said. "It makes no sense for him to go that way. It isn't like the barn is there anymore."

"The barn might not be there anymore, but the cellar is!" Caleb said, as he took off running toward the rubble of the barn.

"Hey," he hollered, as he ran toward the officers. "I think I know where he is!"

He pointed to the hatch from the cellar door. "I think he might be down there."

One of the officers lifted the door and shone his flashlight down in the cellar. "Looks like this rain filled it with water. There's no telling how deep it's gotten, but judging by the flow we can see here, we might not find him alive if he's down there."

Caleb looked at the water draining into the cellar like a sewer on a city street.

The officer hollered into the hole, but Caleb noticed the top rung of the ladder looked freshly broken since the center shade of the wooden step was lighter than the charred outside.

He pointed it out to the officer, and they asked for a volunteer to go down there and look for Zeb.

"I'll go," Caleb offered.

"No, Son," the officer said. "I admire your bravery, but we have special training in emergency situations like this. With all this rain, the walls of that cellar could cave in, and we're better equipped to handle that stuff. Besides, that water is so cold, you could die of hypothermia if you're down there too long."

He motioned for his men to get a cinch collar and straps from the fire truck that had just arrived on the scene.

If he was down there, they might even need to extend the ladder over the opening to pull him and his rescuer out of the flooded cellar.

"I think I found him," the man below shouted up to the others. "No telling if he's alive or not; his face was half in the water, but I think he suffered hypothermia."

The fireman attached the cinch collar around Zeb and yanked on the straps. "Pull him up!"

The officers and fireman pulled on the straps to hoist him out of the cellar, while the fireman in the cellar hung on long enough to get to the ladder that was half-immersed in the cold water from the flooded river.

He watched as they pulled him out and began to revive him. Although Caleb was emotional, he felt a certain numbness to the idea that his father might not survive this. He'd done so much damage to everyone he loved, including himself. He'd probably harmed himself the most by putting more concern on acceptance from the community than he had on doing the right thing.

"We have a pulse," one of them said.

He's breathing on his own, but it's shallow," the other said.

They placed an oxygen mask on his face, but he didn't seem to be conscious. Sadly, Caleb had to wonder if it had been better if they had not tried to revive him.

Chapter 19

Paramedics lifted Seth into an ambulance, an oxygen mask on his face, and a splint on his leg.

He pulled the mask down and looked at Kyle. "I need to tell you something."

"The old man killed my father—Jack. He's in a casket where I was digging. He's also the one who shot me in the arm! I know he's confessed to being my real father, but I'm not like the rest of you. I intend to press charges against him!"

"Let's just concentrate on getting you better first—*brother!*"

"I like the sound of that!" he said, as he replaced the mask on his face and laid back on the stretcher, allowing the paramedics to close the door of the ambulance.

Caleb caught up with him just then, as they wheeled Zeb up on a stretcher.

"How is he?" Kyle asked.

"He's suffered hypothermia from being in the icy water so long, and he may have drowned. They didn't have to jump-start his heart, and he's breathing on his own, but he hasn't been conscious the whole time. How's your cousin?"

"Turns out my *cousin* is our *brother!*"

"You're kidding!"

"Nope! Makes me wonder how many more will turn up."

Caleb slapped Kyle on the back. "I went from being an only child to being part of a baseball team real fast!"

"Except poor Seth looks like the old man!"

"As long as he doesn't act like him, I'll be happy to welcome him into the family. I guess we're going to have to build another house."

Kyle chuckled. "I'd hold off on those plans. Seth is kind of a loner. It might take him longer to get used to the idea than it took for me!"

"Let's go tell the police they have another body to excavate, and then we'll go to the hospital. Seth should be out of surgery by the time we get there."

"We should say a few prayers for him—for both of them."

"I agree," Kyle said. "But let's get the hard part over first."

Caleb couldn't help but think that none of this was going to be easy. Life had certainly thrown them a few curve balls. But really, even that was an understatement.

When they caught up with the officers, they were driving stakes around the property, using trees where available, and even marking off certain areas with yellow tape that read: *Crime Scene Do Not Cross.*

"I'm afraid we have some more evidence you need to be aware of," Kyle began. "Where we found our brother, our old man was making him dig up another body—in the back."

He pointed to where they had just come from.

"I have to warn you that you need to stay off the property now. This is a crime scene, so let us handle everything from here on out. When we showed up here, it wasn't just to arrest Mr. Yoder for escaping. That hair sample you gave us from the funeral of the woman you thought might be the mother of one of you...well, it turns out the DNA doesn't match, which means we have another random murder on our hands."

Caleb felt his world fall out from under him all over again. "If the woman in that grave wasn't my mother, then that means my mother's body is out there missing somewhere."

Kyle patted him on the shoulder. "Or—it could mean she's still alive! Let's try to think positively."

Caleb could feel his heart beating double-time. "With three bodies turning up now, what do you think is the likelihood of her being alive? If she is, why hasn't she tried to contact me all this time?"

"It's possible she could be terrified of the old man, and doesn't dare come around—even if it means losing her son."

Caleb couldn't think about that. He didn't dare hope; didn't dare dream. He'd had to give that up as a child, and he wasn't about to pick it up again now.

Chapter 20

"I know what they told me is probably true," Seth said soberly. "I mean, that's their job to find out the truth, but I find it hard to believe that Jack strangled my mother. They called it a crime of passion."

"Let's not worry about that today, Brother," Kyle said. "Let's give your parents a proper funeral and burial."

The three brothers lifted the handle on one side of his mother's casket, ushers from the church on the other, and brought it to the front of the little white church she used to frequent. Then, they did the same with Jack's casket.

At the back of the church, a woman with short, red hair and dark sunglasses sat in the last pew.

Seth greeted her, introducing her as Rosa, who waited tables at the diner in Hartford.

Caleb shook as he looked at the *English* woman; her short, black dress and long, black coat making her look like a stranger, but he knew her as his mother, Rose.

He flung himself in her arms, and she pulled him close, the two of them sobbing.

"Why did you leave and become *English?*"

"Your father put me under the ban—from you! I'm only dressed this way to keep him from recognizing me. He likes plain, blond women, and this is the exact opposite of what he would pay any attention to. I've kept an eye on you from afar, but I stayed away to protect you. Then, when I read in the paper about all the bodies, and the fact he may never wake up, I figured it was safe to see you. I'm so sorry it had to be this way."

"I understand," he said, sniffling. "I've missed you. I have a lot to tell you. I'm married now, and she's expecting!"

"You mean I'm going to be a *grossmammi?*"

"Jah," he said chuckling. "Come with me, I'd like you to meet Amelia. Do you remember her?"

"I've seen you with her," his mother said. "I'm pleased you and Amelia found each other again after all these years, and I'd love to see her again, but I have to face my sister first. You understand, don't you?"

He kissed her on the cheek and nodded, escorting her to the front of the church, where her sister, Selma, sat with Amelia and her mother.

Chapter 21

The doors at the back of the church burst open suddenly, followed by a lot of gasps and hushed voices, as several police officers walked up the aisle toward the caskets.

"I'm sorry," one of the officers Seth recognized said to him. "But we're going to have to take the woman's body into custody for further investigation."

Seth felt anger rise up in him as he tried to stand between the officers and his mother's casket.

"Why are you doing this? Why would you take my mother's body when I'm about to bury her so she can finally rest in peace?"

The officer laid a hand on his shoulder. "I'm taking the body, because she's not your mother."

Seth felt his legs wobble. Was it possible for the bottom to fall out of his world more than once in the course of two days?

"I can explain," a familiar woman's voice called from the back of the church.

Seth thought he might pass out if he looked at her, but he had to confirm his suspicion. But how? Was this some sort of trick? He'd seen her body with his own eyes.

The sound of her footsteps as she made her way up the aisle filled Seth with a morbid sense of dread. He was too frightened to look; in case it wasn't true.

A soft hand rested on his wounded arm he still had propped in a sling. "I was told he shot you," she said in her soothing, gentle voice. It was the same voice that had calmed him at night when he was a young boy, the same soft voice that would reprimand him with love, and tell him funny stories that had kept him awake at night wanting more instead of putting him to sleep as her intentions were.

It was, without a doubt, the voice of his mother.

Chapter 22

Seth turned to look at her, nearly collapsing when he looked into her familiar blue eyes. He choked down a strangled cry as he pulled his mother into his arms.

"I thought you were dead," he sobbed and laughed at the same time. "I'm so glad I didn't lose you, Mom."

"That woman you were about to bury; she's my sister," his mother said. "She's actually your birth mother, but she's also my twin sister, Beth."

"What are you talking about? I didn't know you had a twin," he said. "Why didn't you ever tell me?"

"It's a long story," she said. "Let's sit down and talk for a minute so I can explain."

He followed her to the back pew where Caleb's mother had just sat only moments ago. That was a shock to him, and now, he knew just how Caleb must have been feeling.

She sat down and faced him, her cheeks tear-stained.

"Jack left me after we had a fight when all this came out just a few months ago, and I've been in hiding this whole time," she explained. "I was embarrassed that Jack had left me because he thought I was lying to him. I was angry with him, and we had words. He said he was leaving me, and there was no reasoning with him. I thought he would come back home after taking a drive to cool off, and we could talk and work things out. In the meantime, I figured I would warn Zeb that Jack had threatened to kill him for taking advantage of me—which never happened."

"Tell me first, how did I get to be your son?" he asked.

"My sister had come to stay with me while Jack was out of town on business. She and I gave birth on the same night, and we were alone with a midwife. My own son was stillborn, and my sister, Beth, also gave birth to a son. She asked me to raise him—you—as my own, because she was a single mother, and the child—you—belonged to Zeb Yoder. She didn't want to raise a child with him because he was a brutal man even then, and we knew of his other indiscretions; it was a small community. So, she replaced my stillborn son as her own and told Zeb the child died so he would leave her alone. But somehow, he found out and threatened to expose us all. He threatened to tell Jack I'd betrayed him, and by that time you were about seven years old, and I'd grown very attached to you. Beth made a decision to visit Zeb once a week to appease him and keep him from revealing the truth. We both accepted the burden to keep peace and to keep you safe."

"That doesn't explain why Jack—dad strangled you—her—my birth mother."

"I went to Zeb to warn him Jack had found out, and he should just come clean with everything, but Beth was already there, and Jack was not thinking straight. He was angry and wouldn't listen to Beth. He accused her as if she was me, making accusations that I'd betrayed him, and said he didn't believe a word I'd said. He even accused me of being with Zeb, and claimed he wondered if the twins were his children. The whole thing was a mess. He fought with Zeb and knocked him out, and then fought with Beth some more, still thinking she was me. Then, he began to strangle her. I screamed, and it distracted him toward me, and that's when Zeb shot him. I ran off before Zeb could catch me, and I went to Florida as planned. I wrote the letter before I left and dropped it in the mailbox, claiming we had been in Florida all that time, and that Jack was with me because I had to get away from Zeb. I was terrified he would find me and come after me and kill me for what I saw."

"Is that why you brought the police here now?"

"I read in the newspaper about the funeral—my funeral and Jack's, and knew you'd be here, devastated. So I went to the police and told them everything."

"So Jack—my dad, really did strangle the woman he thought was you?"

He hung his head, feeling shame that he had two fathers—and both of them were murderers.

She laid a hand on his arm. "Don't let this be a reflection on you," she said gently.

"I wish I'd known her. I wish I'd known Beth."

"You did!" she said. "Every opportunity we were away from the house, she would take my place and spend time with you."

"Didn't Jack know you had a sister?"

She shook her head and lowered her gaze. "She kept her Amish heritage, and became part of another community. I was so busy being an *Englisher* to be with Jack, that we didn't intermingle around him. When we made that pact that night for me to raise you, she never came out in the open again—except to see you."

"It almost seems that she was killed just for being my mother," he said with a deep sadness.

She tucked her finger under his stubbly chin, forcing him to look at her. "It was a burden she was willing to bear. She loved you!"

"But she gave me away."

"She gave you up hoping you would have a better life than being raised by a single mother who was a slave to her sin with Zeb Yoder. That's what killed her; it wasn't because of you."

He rested his head on his mother's shoulder, feeling as if the whole world had turned on him. He struggled to grasp the reality of having his mother back—the woman who had not given birth to him, but had raised him as her own. It was tough for him not to feel like an orphan—even with all his new family around him.

Chapter 23

"Do you think you'll ever get baptized into the church?" Seth asked Caleb.

"Nah. I don't have much faith in their ways now, since they turned their backs on me and Amelia when we were just innocent children. They might have been able to give us some support and even protection, but they were more concerned with banning the family because of our father's sins."

"Not all communities are like this one," Selma offered.

"We have our roots here," he said. "And with the baby coming, we're content to stay in our new home on land we own."

"I know one thing is certain," Seth admitted. "I'm finally going to put my bad-boy days behind me and fulfill the promise I made to my mother. I don't want my bad habits to turn me into the same kind of person the old man was."

"I don't think you have to worry about being anything like him," his mother said. "You've inherited the good from my sister. She would be proud to know the man you've turned out to be. Before she died, she made me promise to get you back on the straight path."

"So that was *her* promise I broke," Seth said with shame. "Don't worry, I'll make her proud of me. I've got two brothers now I thought I'd never have, and they've offered me a place in their business so I can stop the gambling and work for a living, instead of thinking I need everything handed to me."

"That's a good attitude to have, partner," Kyle said, slapping him on the back. "I think this *brother thing* is going to work out for all of us."

"I do too," Caleb said, looking at the large family he'd gained overnight.

Amelia sat with her mother knitting booties for her unborn child. She was perfectly content to stay out of the conversation, being too preoccupied with learning all the things her mother had not been able to teach her in her growing years. But now that she was about to be a mother herself, Amelia was grateful to have the woman there to guide her.

She looked up and smiled.

Yes, her new family was going to be good for the child she carried. She hoped, for her husband's sake that the newest brother, Seth would stay and be part of the family the way he had hopes for it.

Then an idea sparked in her. The best way to get a man to settle down was to find him a good woman, and her cousin, Katie, would be perfect for him.

She giggled at the thought of her child's new *Onkel Seth* wearing Amish clothing, but knew if anyone could get him to do it, Katie could.

THE END

ATTENTION READER: If you have enjoyed this series, and would love for me to continue with more books in the series, please leave a review on Amazon telling me how much you've enjoyed reading them and that you would like more.

Thank you for taking the time to read this new series. I have enjoyed writing it.

Happy Reading!

Made in the USA
Lexington, KY
13 May 2016